P9-BYA-844

For my old friend, Bill Vickery,
and for Jim, who knows the magic

J. L.

For Andy and Pete,
Mannerheim and Schmetz

A. G.

Text copyright © 2001 by Jonathan London
Illustrations copyright © 2001 by Adam Gustavson

All rights reserved. No part of this book may be reproduced, transmitted, or stored in an information retrieval system in any form or by any means, graphic, electronic, or mechanical, including photocopying, taping, and recording, without prior written permission from the publisher.

First edition 2001

Library of Congress Cataloging-in-Publication Data
London, Jonathan, date.
Where the big fish are / Jonathan London ; illustrated by Adam Gustavson. — 1st ed.
p. cm.
Summary: Although their efforts to build a raft so they can go "where the big fish are" are almost destroyed by a fierce storm, two young boys do not give up.
ISBN 0-7636-0922-6
[1. Rafts—Fiction. 2. Fishing—Fiction.
3. Perseverance (Ethics)—Fiction.] I. Gustavson, Adam, ill. II. Title.
PZ7.L8432 Raf 2001
[Fic]—dc21 00-025919

2 4 6 8 10 9 7 5 3 1

Printed in Hong Kong

This book was typeset in Journal. The illustrations were done in oil.

Candlewick Press
2067 Massachusetts Avenue
Cambridge, Massachusetts 02140

Where the Big Fish Are

Jonathan London · illustrated by Adam Gustavson

CANDLEWICK PRESS
CAMBRIDGE, MASSACHUSETTS

We talk about it all summer. About going out to where the really big fish are. Then one day, tired of saying, "If we had a raft . . ."

I jump up and say, “Let’s go!”

We tear back up the slope behind the dock.
I can hear Bill huffing behind me.
“Used to be tracks around here,” I yell.

“Wait up, will ya!” Bill pants.

“Railroad tracks,” I say.

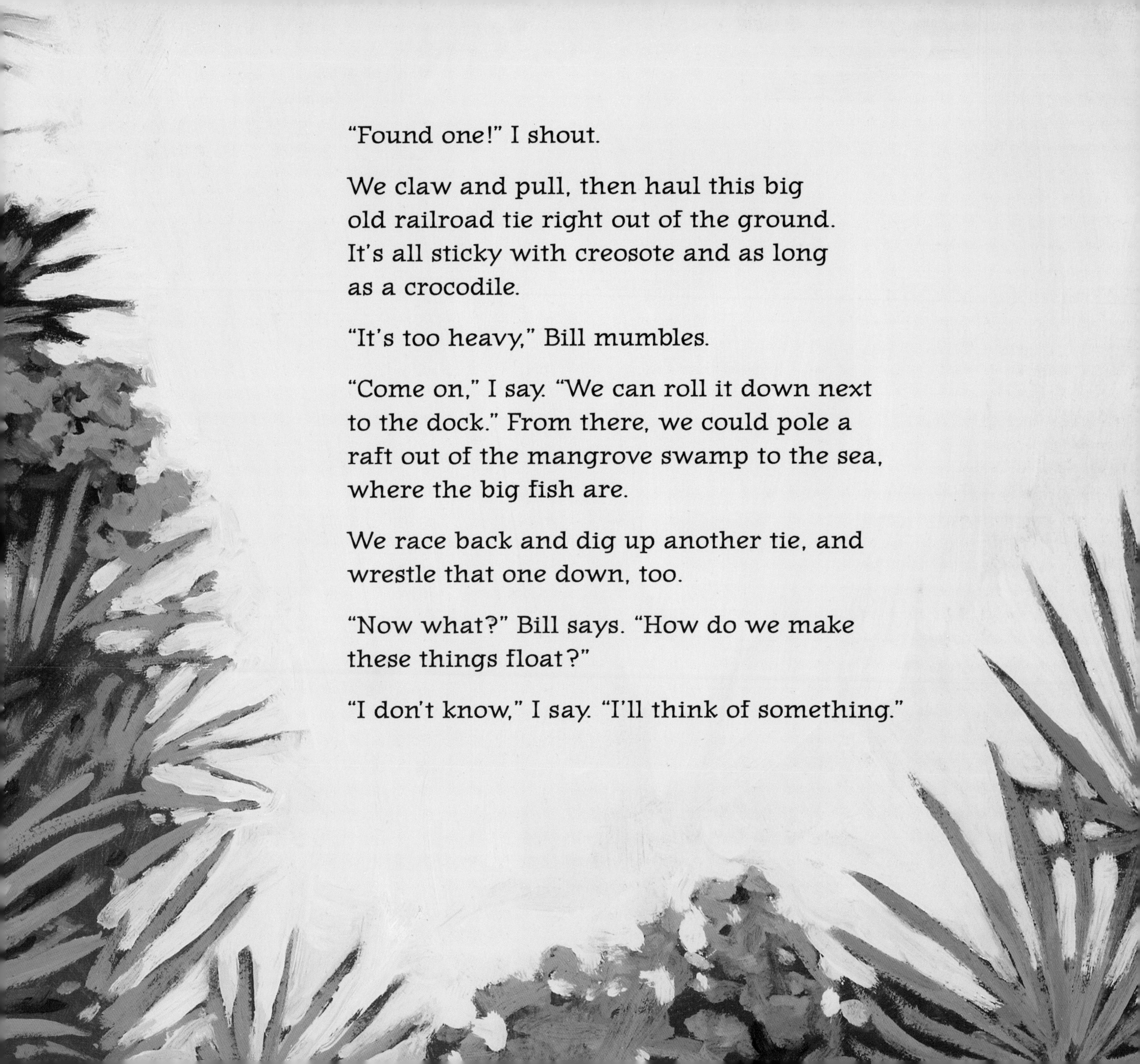

"Found one!" I shout.

We claw and pull, then haul this big old railroad tie right out of the ground. It's all sticky with creosote and as long as a crocodile.

"It's too heavy," Bill mumbles.

"Come on," I say. "We can roll it down next to the dock." From there, we could pole a raft out of the mangrove swamp to the sea, where the big fish are.

We race back and dig up another tie, and wrestle that one down, too.

"Now what?" Bill says. "How do we make these things float?"

"I don't know," I say. "I'll think of something."

At supper, I make
a raft on my plate
with fish sticks
and French fries.
"Quit playing
with your food!"
Mom says.

Then she brings
out doughnuts
for dessert.

Next morning,
I sprint to Bill's
house.

"Wake up!
Wake up!"

He grumbles
and groans.

"Inner tubes,"
I whisper.

"What the . . . ?"

"Inner tubes!"

For a handful
of quarters,
we get a deal
from the junk
man on two
huge airplane
inner tubes.
They're full of
holes, but we
patch them up—
and roll them
along like giant
black doughnuts.

Back at the dock, Bill starts lashing the inner tubes between the ties with rope, and I nail down some old warped boards.

Bill sweats like crazy—and gets a splinter in his thumb—"Ouch!" He's about ready to quit, but when I start talking about fishing, he starts wrestling with that rope again.

After that, Bill finds an old flagpole. "Think this will work as a mast?" he asks. We rig it up, then shove the raft in and tie it to the dock.

"Hey, it floats!" Bill hollers. He's so excited he does a little dance.

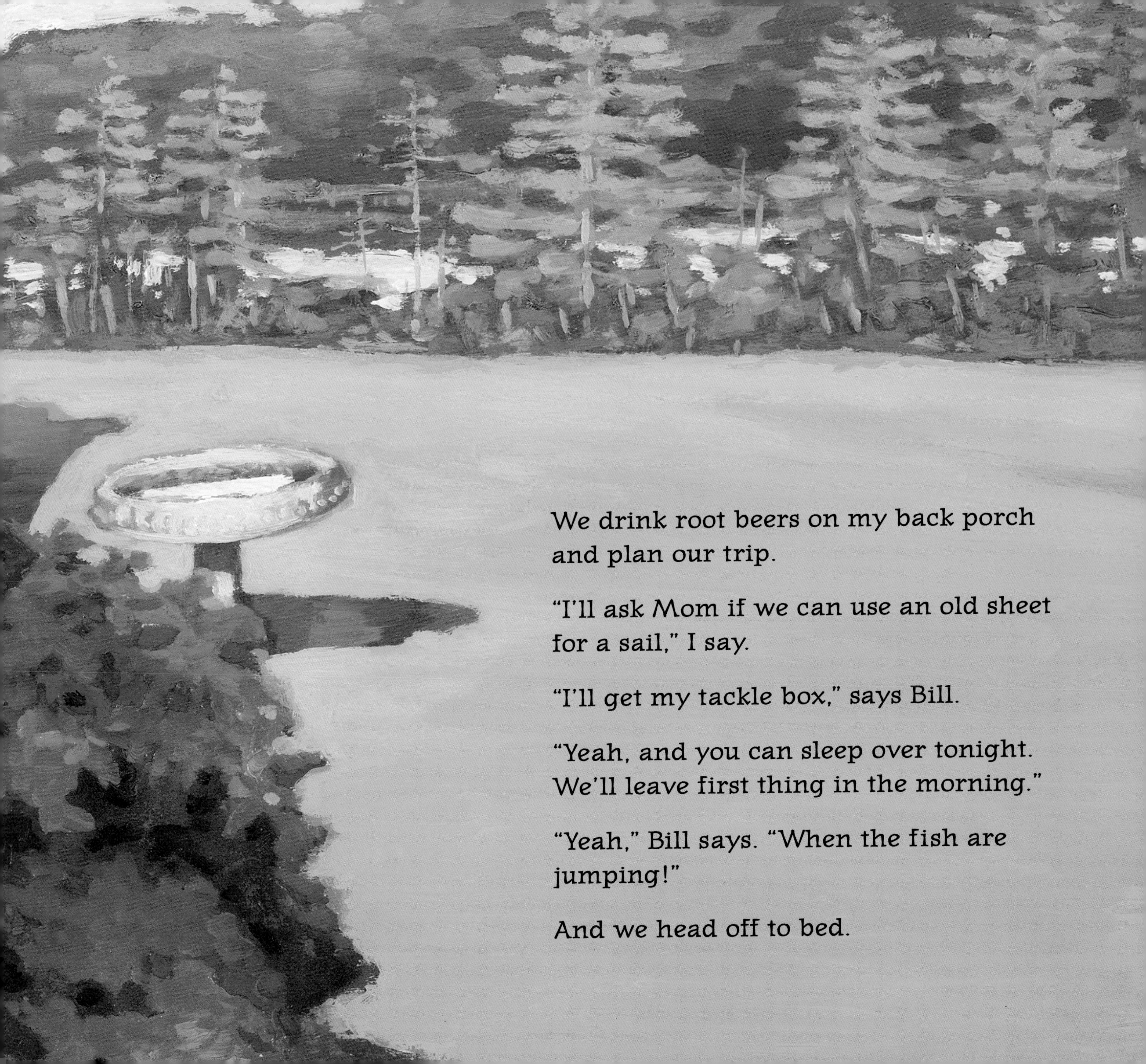

We drink root beers on my back porch and plan our trip.

"I'll ask Mom if we can use an old sheet for a sail," I say.

"I'll get my tackle box," says Bill.

"Yeah, and you can sleep over tonight. We'll leave first thing in the morning."

"Yeah," Bill says. "When the fish are jumping!"

And we head off to bed.

The first drops hit the windows around midnight, hard as pebbles. It's like a hurricane outside. The wind slams sledgehammers into the house.

I look over at Bill's sleeping bag. He's gone.

The raft! I think, and tear outside.

Down in the swamp I see the raft crashing
around at the end of the dock.
And there's Bill, hanging on to the rope
like he's hauling in a huge fish.

"Bill!" I shout.

Just as I get to him,
the rope snaps—but
Bill hangs on—and
I do a flying tackle.
The rope whips loose
from his hands, and
the raft disappears
into the storm.

In the morning, the sky is scrubbed clean.
We slip and slide in the mud and climb
over blasted trees, searching for the raft.

"It's a goner," I say.

And then we find it. What's left. It's a wreck.
It's totaled. We just stand there and stare at
our shattered raft. I feel like a popped balloon.

But Bill, he's like a turtle, slow but sure. He turns to me and says, "Aw crud, better get our hammers." I look at him like he's nuts. "Those fish are just waiting!" he says.

Then we get to work. We pick up the best of the busted boards, straighten bent and twisted nails, and fix everything the storm has broken.

When we're done, we push our raft back into the water and grab our stuff and hop aboard. It tips. We almost fall . . . then catch our balance.

"Let's go fishing!" Bill shouts.

Then we slowly pole our way out
of the mangrove swamp to the sea,
where the big fish are.

"I bet I'll catch the biggest fish," I say.
But I'm just joking. I bet Bill catches
the biggest one today.